little *zoé*

Bloomers

childrens dresswear & gifts

Nana — 1998
RIVERSIDE, CA

MEG'S DEAREST WISH

THE LITTLE WOMEN JOURNALS™
by *Charlotte Emerson*
from *Avon Books*

Madame Alexander®
ALEXANDER DOLL COMPANY, INC.

The Little Women Journals™

—— MEG'S DEAREST WISH ——

Charlotte Emerson

Illustrations by Kevin Wasden

AVON BOOKS ◆ NEW YORK

AVON BOOKS
A division of
The Hearst Corporation
1350 Avenue of the Americas
New York, New York 10019

Library of Congress Cataloging in Publication Data:

Emerson, Charlotte.
   Meg's dearest wish / Charlotte Emerson.—1st ed.
      p.   cm.—(Little women journals)
Summary: Initially delighted when she receives an invitation to wealthy and elegant Lily
Pomeray's house party, Meg is mortified to learn that she has not been invited as a guest
but rather to help make the costumes for a masquerade.
[1. Friendship—Fiction. 2. Conduct of life—Fiction. 3. Sisters—Fiction. 4. Family
life—New England—Fiction. 5. New England—Fiction.] I. Alcott, Louisa May,
1832–1888. Little women. II. Title. III. Series: Emerson, Charlotte. Little women
journals.
PZ7.E5835Me   1997   97-7274
[Fic]—dc21   CIP

First Avon Books Printing: February 1998

AVON TRADEMARK REG. U.S. PAT. OFF. AND IN OTHER COUNTRIES, MARCA REGISTRADA, HECHO EN
U.S.A.

Printed in the U.S.A.

FIRST EDITION

QPM   10   9   8   7   6   5   4   3   2

TABLE OF CONTENTS

CONTENTS

MEG'S DEAREST WISH

CHAPTER ONE

————— ⚬⚬ —————

Indian Summer

"*I*f one must do a chore on such a beautiful day, then apple picking is just the thing," Jo March observed cheerfully. She swung her basket energetically, hitting her sister Meg on the knee.

"Jo, take care," Meg scolded. She reached up to straighten her bonnet.

"There's not a soul around, Meg," Jo said, breaking into a run. "Isn't this glorious!" she shouted behind her.

"Wait for me, Jo!" Amy cried. Dropping her basket, eleven-year-old Amy raced after her sister.

Beth laughed. "Catch her, Amy!" she cheered.

"Follow me, girls!" Jo cried. She jumped over a ladder lying on the grass, danced around an over-turned basket, and swung from a low-hanging branch with a whoop. Amy followed, trying to keep up with her tall, lanky sister.

Meg should have scolded Jo again. At sixteen she felt it was her duty, as the eldest of four sisters, to correct undignified behavior. But Amy and Jo were having such fun, and Beth was laughing so hard, that Meg couldn't help but join in.

And Jo was right. It *was* a glorious day!

"Come on, Beth," Meg urged. Picking up her skirts, she ran after Jo and Amy. Beth only hesitated a moment before following her, dodging apple trees, fallen fruit, and baskets.

The four sisters ended up sitting on the grass, short of breath and laughing.

"I can't remember the last time I ran like that," Meg said breathlessly. "I know I'm much too old to do such a thing, but I couldn't help it."

"Good for you," Jo said. "Well, I think Beth won the romp. She's the only one of us who kept all her apples in her basket."

The other girl laughed. It was true. Although

Beth had lagged behind them, she was the only one to have kept her basket on her arm, and it was still filled with the apples she'd picked.

"I shall make you a crown, my lady," Jo said, her brown eyes twinkling. She leaned over to pick some goldenrod.

Meg looked up at the blue sky and puffy white clouds. The sweet smell of ripe apples wafted on the breeze. It was an unseasonably warm day for autumn. Though only yesterday they had worn scarves and gloves, today Meg had dressed in her summer gingham dress and her shawl.

"Do you remember when we owned this or-chard, Jo?" Meg asked. "We used to picnic here. I remember one day in the spring, when the trees were full of blossoms. We had a whole roast chicken, sweet butter and rolls, cheese, and choco-late cake."

Jo frowned over the garland she was fashioning. "I don't remember, Meg."

"Father was so handsome," Meg went on. "And Mother wore a blue silk dress."

"Marmee had a blue silk dress?" Amy asked, her blue eyes round. She was always interested in clothes. "I wish she'd kept it!"

Meg sighed. "She made it over for Cousin Letty when she married. Letty couldn't afford a wedding dress."

"That's just like Marmee," Beth said softly.

"And who needs a silk dress, anyway?" Jo said, scowling over the flowers in her lap.

"I do," Amy said mournfully.

"You're too young, Amy," Meg said. "I'm the eldest."

"Someday I'll buy you a silk dress, Meg," Jo told her, waving a stalk of goldenrod. "When I'm famous and rich. What color would you like? How about a deep, devastating ruby? And your lace shall positively drip off the sleeves!"

Meg smiled at Jo, but her heart felt sore. She was so weary of talking about the nice things they might have someday. It was all a collection of pretty dreams, for the Marches were poor and likely to continue to be so. That thought made Meg feel even sadder, for as the eldest she remembered better times.

Once, the March family had been comfortable. There was plenty of food to eat, and fires blazed in every room. Meg remembered Christmases that were a blur of brightly wrapped presents, ribbons, and plates of sweet things to eat. They hadn't been rich like their neighbors, the Laurences, but they hadn't suffered from want, and they had plenty to share.

The memories made her feel melancholy, but still she kept them close to her heart. They were already fading. At fifteen, Jo was only a year younger than she, but Jo claimed to barely remember a time when ease and plenty were a part of their lives. And Jo didn't like to look back, at any rate. "Charge ahead!" Jo would say if Meg yearned for the past. "That's my motto, Meg!"

Jo finished twining the goldenrod and placed it on Beth's dark hair. "There you are, my queen," she said.

"Make *me* one, Jo," Amy begged.

Jo rose with an *oof.* "I'd love to, Amy, but we'd better finish picking. The afternoon is slipping away." Jo held out a hand to help Amy up. "You're still a princess, my dear. Tomorrow I shall make you a crown of bright autumn leaves."

Satisfied, Amy rose. "I dropped all my apples," she said with a sigh. "It was fun to pick them at first. But now it seems like a chore again."

"I'll tell you what, Amy," Meg said. "Let's see who can pick the most beautiful red apple. Then later you can sketch it, and we'll have a memory of this perfect day."

"If I have any time to sketch after having to make applesauce and apple butter and apple pies," Amy grumbled.

"I'm looking forward to the baking," Beth said softly. "Cinnamon and cloves and apples make the house smell so good."

"And you know that's our agreement with Mr. Crockett," Meg told Amy. "Marmee would only agree to his generous offer to pick as much as we like if we send over applesauce and pies to him. He's all alone, you know."

"It's so sad to be alone," Beth said.

"Not necessarily," said Jo. "Think of the freedom. No one to account to."

"And the last piece of pie would always be yours!" Amy added.

"Enough chatter!" Meg teased. "If we don't finish our picking, there shall be no apple pies for anyone."

Amy ran off to retrieve her basket and find the reddest apple, and Beth wandered off to fill her apron with more. As Meg began to pick apples from a low branch, she thought of the old days when the orchard belonged to the March family and they didn't need permission to pick from its trees.

"I've got to stop wishing for things I can't have," she scolded herself as she dropped a shiny apple in her basket. "I must remember my blessings, as Marmee says. What are fine silk dresses next to a happy home?"

Just then a trill of laughter rippled across the orchard. Meg stopped, her hand in the air. It wasn't the merry laughter of her sisters. She peeked around the tree trunk.

Four girls walked down the adjoining meadow. Ribbons fluttered, parasols swayed, and silk skirts trailed on the grass.

Meg recognized the group immediately. Who could miss Lily Pomeray's shining raven hair and elegant carriage? With her were two young ladies Meg didn't know, and Sallie Gardiner, one of Meg's closest friends.

A pang shot through Meg. Sallie hadn't called on her for the past couple of weeks, and Meg had heard how Lily Pomeray had swept her up in her set. Miss Pomeray had moved to Concord only recently. She'd immediately established herself as the wittiest, brightest, most elegant young lady in town. It was whispered that Belle Moffat was furiously jealous of Miss Pomeray's social success.

Meg studied Lily's silk gown, striped in various ravishing shades of green. Her parasol was of the palest pink, and a silk fringed shawl in tones of pink and green trailed from Lily's narrow shoulders. It dragged behind her on the grass, but Lily didn't seem to mind. She most likely had drawers full of such elegant shawls, Meg thought enviously.

Suddenly she became aware of her summer gingham, so comfortable but so inappropriate on an autumn day, no matter how warm. She had worn her favorite old bonnet, and it was terribly ordinary. And she hadn't even worn her gloves!

Meg's critical glance swept to her sisters. Jo had insisted on wearing her broad-brimmed riding hat so that the sun wouldn't get in her eyes. It looked ridiculous with her maroon everyday gown. And she had a grass stain on the back of her skirt!

Beth had removed her apron and was using it as a basket for more apples. She looked sweet and modest as usual, but the goldenrod Jo had twined through her hair lent her a comical air.

At least Amy looked her usual neat and pretty self, Meg supposed. But right now her youngest sister was up a tree, squirming to reach a bright red apple.

Meg couldn't be introduced to Lily Pomeray this way! She wished she were wearing the new lilac coat she was so proud of. And she even had a brand new muff, thanks to Aunt March's generosity. It would be much easier to face Lily Pomeray armed with her new muff made of soft white fur.

Lifting her skirts, Meg dashed toward her sisters. "Jo!" she called urgently in a low voice. "Jo!"

Jo looked up from her basket, where she was searching for the most perfect apple. "What is it? You might want to rest a bit, Meg, you look all flushed and queer."

"Jo," Meg whispered, stepping behind a tree trunk, "keep your voice down. Sallie Gardiner is over by the edge of the orchard, and I don't want her to see us."

Jo craned her neck to glimpse Meg's friend. "Whyever not? She could help us pick apples."

"No!" Meg cried. She lowered her voice. "She's with Miss Pomeray. She's become her particular friend. I'm dying to meet her, but not like this." Meg looked down at her gown. To her dismay, she noticed that her hem was dirty.

Jo peered round the tree trunk. "Miss Pomeray . . . Is she the one with the dark hair and that silly bonnet?" At Meg's nod, Jo wrinkled her nose. "Oh, Meg. You don't care to meet such silly people, do you?"

"Of course I do. She's very elegant and fascinating," Meg said, peering round the tree with Jo. "Look at her gown!"

"I could do with less ribbons and ruffles, but you don't care for my opinion when it comes to dress," Jo said critically. She dusted off her hands on her skirt.

Noticing their two sisters in conversation, Beth and Amy had drawn closer.

"Who is that elegant girl?" Amy said breathily, leaning against the tree trunk to stare at Lily. "Oh, Meg, what a bonnet she's got on! I wish I had ribbons trailing down my back, don't you? I think you're much prettier, though," she said loyally, with a heartfelt smile at Meg.

"I haven't seen Sallie for ever so long," Meg mused. "I suppose Lily Pomeray is more amusing to be around."

Jo slipped an arm around her sister. "Impossible," she said stoutly. "Sallie is a fool to treat your friendship lightly. I like her, but the girl can be an awful goose."

"A good friend will always return," Beth said. "She is most likely trying to make Miss Pomeray feel welcome."

"Oh, they're looking this way!" Meg cried, ducking again behind the tree. "Don't let them see us!"

Jo flattened herself against the trunk. "You are being a terrible bother, Meg. Why don't you just walk over and shake hands like a man?"

"Oh, Jo, you don't understand," Meg said, fretfully biting her lip.

Amy peeked around the tree. "They're going toward the river, Meg."

The four sisters popped out from behind the sturdy tree. They all gave a last look at the elegant group now sweeping down the hill toward the blue river.

"What a ridiculous set," Jo said, pushing her hat down firmly on her head. "You tell me this Miss Pomeray is elegant, Meg, and I suppose I'll have to believe you. But in my opinion, wearing that delicate silk on such a changeable day is just plain silly. And if you did go around with such a set, you'd have all sorts of trouble trying to keep up. You'd start worrying about how many pairs of gloves you have, and if your bonnet is this year's fashion. What an almighty bother!"

As Jo tramped off to find her basket, Meg turned away with a sigh.

Everything Jo said was most likely true. But it didn't help cheer her one bit. Meg *did* want to be accepted by Lily's set.

She leaned over to pick up her basket, which suddenly seemed a heavy burden. Before the Marches had lost their wealth, she would have been among Lily's group. She would have been stepping along in fine kid boots and a ravishing bonnet, having nothing to do on a fine day but laugh and chatter. Instead, she was picking apples and wearing a very ordinary dress and a very old bonnet.

And no matter how she scolded her foolish heart, she knew that her dearest wish was to take her place in that fine society—and belong there.

CHAPTER TW

— ⚬❧⚬ —

Paris Fashion

"*H*ail, postmistress!" Jo called to Beth the next day. "Anything for me?"

"A letter from Laurie," Beth answered, her hands full of envelopes and a small bouquet. It was her job to check the mailbox that their young neighbor, Theodore Laurence, had placed in the hedge between their properties. Letters and clippings, sheets of music and poems, fruit and sweet things were passed back and forth between the two houses.

Beth's rosy face glowed with pleasure. "Such

13

ures today! A bouquet for Marmee, a new draw-
g pencil for Amy, peppermints for me—I'll
share!—and a package for Meg."

"A package?" Meg looked up from her sewing.
"What did the boy send me? Something to tease
me, most likely."

Beth placed the small bouquet in a vase near
Marmee's corner. Then she handed Meg her package. Meg unwound the string and unwrapped the
brown paper. Inside she found a stack of magazines.

Meg laughed. "These are in French! Laurie is
such a tease. He was horrid to me about my accent
the other day. I suppose this is a hint for me to
practice." Meg's dark brown curls brushed against
her cheeks as she bent over the papers.

"What are they?" Jo asked round a mouthful of
peppermints.

"Wait, there's a letter enclosed," Meg said. "Let
me read it:

Dear Meg,

*My cousin Winifred, who lives in Paris and is
quite stylish, I assure you, sent these along after a
request from me. I thought you might enjoy a glimpse*

14

of Paris modes. I guarantee that these are the most up-to-the-minute styles!

Your humble servant,
Laurie

"French fashion!" Meg cried. "Come look, girls. *Le Magasin des Demoiselles.* Oh, bless the boy!"

Amy hurried over, but Jo returned to her book with a hearty "Oh, pshaw!" Though she wasn't interested in fashion, Beth followed Amy. She held out the bag of peppermints to Meg and leaned over her chair to examine the drawings.

"What does it say?" Amy asked eagerly. "Read the descriptions, Meg. I'm sure they're as elegant as the gowns."

"Let me puzzle it out," Meg said, frowning. " 'This bodice of pearl-colored silk is laced with silk ribbon in the back, thereby reducing the apparent size of the waist.' "

"It's lovely," Amy said. "Look at the wide sleeves. And I like those short gloves with bracelets."

"The basque is so long and pointed," Meg mused. "That would make the waist look smaller, too."

"What's *trente-et-sept?*" Amy wondered.

"Thirty-seven," Jo piped up from the couch. "Which you should know, if you studied properly."

"Thirty-seven yards of tulle," Meg said breathily. "Can you imagine?"

"How elegant," Amy said approvingly.

"How I wish I had Belgian lace!" Meg said with a sigh.

"How I wish I had a bonnet with feathers!" Amy said, her sigh echoing Meg's.

Jo looked at them over her book. "How I wish I could wear a serviceable pair of trousers with plenty of room to stride, and ride, and turn somersaults if I wanted to!"

Busy studying the drawings, Meg barely heard Jo. She turned over the leaves of the magazine eagerly. She was in the middle of trimming a new party dress, and her mind was suddenly crowded with fresh ideas.

"Maybe a narrower sash is the thing," she wondered aloud. "And I'm sure I could find some spring green velvet ribbons just like those. Or perhaps lilac."

Lost in dreams of elegance, Meg hadn't noticed that Jo had risen. She took a piece of string and tied Beth's little red pillow on top of her head. Then she tucked a pussy willow branch underneath like a jaunty feather. Wrapping a worn quilt around her waist like a skirt, Jo added the final touch: Marmee's tiny bouquet, which she tucked into her collar underneath her chin.

"*Regardez*, la-deez," Jo trilled, striking a pose. "Ze latest fashion of Paree!"

Meg had thought she was too mature and dignified to ever engage in a pillow fight again. But as she grabbed a tapestry pillow and fired it at her mischievous sister, she decided that immaturity had its uses. Especially when one had such excellent aim!

CHAPTER THREE

Friendly Favors

Over the next few weeks, Meg studied the French magazines in every spare moment. Even with her limited purse, she was still able to adapt some of the ideas she found there. It was so satisfying how such simple matters as the width of a ribbon or the addition of a ruffle could make such a difference!

Soon Meg began to hear whispers around Concord to the effect that "Meg March has elegant taste."

Meg knew that Jo thought her new attention to

fashion was a frivolous pursuit. Marmee merely shook her head and smiled. She was most likely letting Meg "have her head," as Jo might say. Sometimes, even if Marmee thought one was going a bit astray, she found it better to say nothing and let one figure things out for oneself.

But I can't help caring about clothes! Meg wrote in her journal.

> *Even if I am a poor man's daughter, I still want to look as well as I can. And people aren't admiring me because I spend money on clothes, but rather because I use my imagination to improve what I have.*
>
> *So what could possibly be wrong with that?*

"It's all your fault, Teddy," Jo told Laurie one evening as they sat outside on a blanket in the garden, bundled against the chill. Laurie had called on Jo and Meg with an armful of oranges and an invitation to "Come outside, will you, you must watch this sunset, it's positively Parisian!"

"You're the one who filled Meg's head with all that fussy French nonsense," Jo went on.

"I'm having fun, and using my hands and imagination to do it," Meg said, defending herself.

"I think she looks charming," Laurie said. "It isn't as though she looks grand and yet silly at the same time, like Belle Moffat. She still looks like our modest Meg."

"I know you look pretty, Meg," Jo said. "You always do. But when your head is full of ruffles and lace, it's hard for a body to have a decent chat with you. You look up and say, 'Excuse me? Did you say something?' after I've been rattling on for a half hour."

"Hmmmm," Meg said as she peeled an orange. "Does such distracted behavior remind you of anyone else, Laurie?"

Laurie pretended to knit his thick black brows. "Let me think. Hmmmm . . . could it be . . . Jo March?" His black eyes twinkled merrily at Jo.

"Me?" Jo asked, astonished. "Since when is my head filled with ruffles and feathers?"

"Perhaps not ruffles and feathers," Laurie said, laughing. "But characters and plots. How many times have I been rattling on to you about something or other, and then you fix me with your brown eyes and say, 'What was that, Teddy? I was just wondering if Angelo should drown, or swim safely to shore with Eugenia.'"

Meg and Laurie laughed heartily at this familiar picture. Jo's face flushed, but then she burst out laughing along with them.

"I suppose you're right," she told them. "But I do think it terribly rude of both of you to turn the tables."

Meg began to pull apart her orange. "Don't you see, Jo, that making over my dresses is fun for me? The same way that you like to write, and Amy likes to sketch. I don't ask you not to scribble away up in the garret, you know."

"Bless you, Meg, you're right," Jo declared. "I'll not say another word. Sew feathers on your boots and hang beads from your bonnets. My lips are sealed."

Laurie handed Jo a fruit section. "Don't seal them yet, old chap. You haven't finished your orange."

"Oh, bother, there's someone at the door," Jo said the next day. "I only just started to roll out this pie dough, and I'm covered in flour."

"I have to peel the apples," Beth said quickly, for it was the usual time for callers, and she disliked entertaining.

"I'll go," Meg said, whipping off her apron. She patted at her hair as she hurried to the front door.

Sallie Gardiner stood on the front stoop, shaking rain off her umbrella. She smiled when she saw Meg.

"Meg! I'm glad you're home. I haven't called in so long—"

"Welcome, Sallie," Meg said, standing aside. "Hurry and get out of that cold rain."

"I was afraid I had missed you," Sallie said, removing her coat.

"Jo is in the middle of baking apple pies," Meg explained. "Come into the parlor and I'll get us some tea."

"Oh, I've had my tea, Meg, thank you," Sallie said, perching on a chair. "I have come to ask you a question."

Meg sat opposite her friend. She folded her hands, already smiling in advance of the question. She had a good idea of what it would be. Every year Sallie invited her special girlfriends to an elegant tea in honor of her birthday. It was an invitation Meg always looked forward to. Though the Gardiners were rich, their house wasn't grand like the Moffats'. And though the tea usually involved elegant fare such as lobster salad and cream cakes, Meg never felt too shabby to enjoy herself.

Sallie's thin face looked shy. "Well, actually, I've come to ask a favor, I should say."

Meg gave an encouraging nod, for Sallie seemed hesitant.

"Can you help me look elegant?" Sallie blurted out. "Lately, I've noticed how your gowns look so fresh and pretty. And I love how you arranged your hair the other day at Betsy Villard's tea. I just yearn to look as grown up as Lily Pomeray. Every time I see her, I feel so old-fashioned and drab."

"Nonsense, Sallie, you always look fine," Meg said soothingly. "But of course I'll help, if I can." Meg felt flattered by Sallie's request. Sallie had three times as many gowns and bonnets as Meg, and could afford dozens more. The fact that she had come to Meg for advice pleased her.

"Thank you, Meg," Sallie said, breaking into a smile. "I knew you'd help me! You see, Father refuses to buy me a new gown. But Mother says I can spend some money on new trimming and make one over."

"You mean your pink gown?" Meg asked Sallie.

"Yes, that old thing," Sallie said with a sigh.

Meg reflected that Sallie's dress was less than

six months old. Meg had trimmed and re-trimmed her tarlatan dress for three years now.

But Meg rarely allowed herself to compare herself to her richer friends. It just made her feel gloomy. She'd rather make the most of what she had, and help Sallie to do the same.

Laurie had brought her the newest issue of *Le Magasin* just yesterday. In it was a design of velvet leaves sewn onto the sheer illusion overskirt of a pale silk dress similar to Sallie's.

Meg leaned forward and took Sallie's gloved hands in hers. "I think I can help you," she said.

Sallie brought Meg a length of beautiful rose-colored velvet. Meg set to work cutting out the velvet in the shape of tiny rosebuds. It was tedious work, but Meg employed Amy's nimble fingers to help.

"All we need to do is scatter them on the transparent overskirt," Meg explained. "Sallie is hunting for satin in the same shade, which I'll make into a new sash. Then all I have to do is widen the sleeves a touch and add a fluted ruffle to the bodice."

"It's going to be such a beautiful gown." Amy

sighed. "It's a pity you're not going to be the one to wear it, Meg."

"Pink suits Sallie better," Meg said, her head bent over her work. "She's got such a pale complexion and light hair."

"Is she getting silk boots to match?" Amy wondered. "With French heels?"

"I expect so," Meg said, finishing a rosebud and setting it aside. "But I did tell her to wear only fresh flowers for ornament. Pale pink roses, I thought, or perhaps white with a few green ferns. Marmee says fresh flowers are best, and I agree."

"The gown seems terribly fancy for a tea," Amy observed. She considered herself quite an expert lately, due to the presence of French magazines in the house.

"I heard that Sallie is planning something different for her birthday this year," Meg told her. "She *is* going to be sixteen. Amelia Reston told me that Sallie is going to take just a few particular friends to a concert in Boston—and then dinner in a restaurant!"

Amy dropped her work in her lap in astonishment. "Oh, Meg, how grand! What will you wear?"

"I'm glad I have my lilac coat and muff," Meg

said. "I thought perhaps I could trim my tarlatan in time with some fresh ribbon. Of course, Sallie hasn't invited me yet."

"She shall," Amy said. "She invites you every year. Most likely when she picks up her gown."

"Most likely," Meg agreed. She smoothed the velvet in her lap. "I can't wait to see how she looks in it."

Sallie twirled in front of the mirror. "It's perfect," she said breathlessly. "Oh, Meg, it's so delicate. It's simple, but it makes me feel like an angel."

"You look like one," Meg said, beaming. The pink and rose of the gown cast a glow on Sallie's usually pale white skin, and made her flaxen hair gleam.

"I was thinking of a bright color for a new gown, like Lily wears. But this suits me better, I think," Sallie said. "And Mother will lend me her cameo to wear. Thank you so much."

"It was my pleasure," Meg assured her.

"Wait until Lily sees it!" Sallie exulted. Then suddenly, she blushed and looked away. "Oh, look at the time!" she exclaimed, flustered. "Mother will

be wondering where I am. Can you help me out of this, Meg?"

Meg unbuttoned and unlaced Sallie from the gown. By the time she'd packed it carefully in a box, Sallie was dressed and had her bonnet on.

"I do hate to rush, but I'm so terribly late," Sallie said, avoiding Meg's eyes. "Thank you so much, Meg."

"You're very welcome, Sallie," Meg said, puzzled at her friend's behavior. Sallie had two spots of color high on her cheeks, and she seemed anxious to be away.

Meg walked to the front door and watched her hurry down the lane. Sallie had been in such a rush that she'd forgotten to invite Meg to her birthday outing. And something was bothering her friend— that was clear.

"I wonder what it is," Meg said to herself as she rolled up a stray ribbon. "Perhaps I'll learn whatever it is, by and by."

Meg waited for her invitation. She moved her chair closer to the window so that she could look up from her sewing whenever a coach drove past. Each one was certain to be the Gardiners' driver come to deliver Sallie's note. Every clip-clop of horses' hooves held potential . . . promise . . . hope . . .

Yet each coach drove past without turning toward Orchard House.

As the days wore on, Meg felt sure that there'd been some mistake. Perhaps a servant had misplaced the invitations—but that couldn't be true. Yesterday at the market she'd heard that Cora Goodchurch had received her invitation.

When Sallie's birthday arrived and she still had not received a card, Meg realized that her waiting had been in vain. She'd been excluded from the outing. Now she knew why Sallie's manner had been so odd the day of her visit.

Meg resolved to say nothing to her family. But at teatime, Jo burst into the house and threw off her bonnet.

"Sallie invited Lily Pomeray and Cora Good-church to Boston!" she exclaimed. "Meg, she left you out for her new, fashionable friends!"

Amy and Beth looked up, shocked. Marmee gave an anxious look at Meg.

Meg bent over her knitting. "I know, Jo."

"I think it abominable behavior," Jo said, her

hands on her hips. "How can you sit there and be so calm?"

"What would you like me to do?" Meg asked mildly. "Sallie has a right to issue her own invitations."

"But it's so unfair!" Jo sputtered.

"It's not like Sallie to be unkind," Beth put in.

"Most likely she was only allowed to choose two friends," Meg said, for she'd thought the matter over. "And Lily would want her special friend, Cora, along. She isn't acquainted with me yet."

"It isn't Lily's part, it's Sallie's," Jo said, sitting on the sofa and tapping her foot in irritation. "And I must say, I think it dreadful of Sallie to have you spend all that time dressing her up and then not invite you along."

Meg was glad to have the knitting in her hands. Her eyes stung, for she had felt hurt by the same thought.

But she'd tried to understand Sallie's dilemma and forgive her friend. Sallie struggled with her own jealousy of Annie Moffat, who was prettier and had crowds of fashionable friends. Meg had reasoned that Lily Pomeray's attentions had been hard for Sallie to resist.

But what of my *friendship?* Meg wondered, blinking

back tears. It wasn't fair of Sallie to have used Meg's expertise to win acceptance from other girls. Even if I used my skills to gain popularity with Sallie, Meg thought.

She had gone round and round about the subject for days. But now she contented herself with saying to her sisters, "I didn't help her in order for her to return the favor."

Meg looked up and met Marmee's warm gaze. She was glad she hadn't spoken her dark thoughts aloud.

"That's what makes your kindness all the more valuable, Meg," Marmee said. "I'm proud of you."

"Well, Marmee, I'm sure you're both correct," Jo grumbled. "But I still think our Meg should have been asked to Boston."

Meg bent her head again. But her heart cried out, *So do I, Jo!*

CHAPTER FOUR

Lily Pomeray Pays a Call

"*L*ook at this red curtain!" Jo called to Meg. "Won't it make a smashing cape for Audacia?"

"It's perfect," Meg agreed.

The two girls stood in the living room, surrounded by remnants from an upended rag bag. They had been a gift from the Reverend Alliston. He had heard from Marmee that the girls were putting on a theatrical for the neighborhood children, and had donated the rectory rag bag in case any fabrics could be fashioned into costumes.

Jo had donned her russet leather boots, for she would be playing the duke, and needed to "get in a dukish sort of mood." She added a red velvet nightcap and then painted on a mustache.

"I wonder if this scrap of blue cloth would do for Audacia in the wedding scene," Meg wondered, holding it up. "We're using a sheet for the gown, but we need a veil. Perhaps if we used pretty blue paper . . ."

"What I need is a commanding hat," Jo declared. "I wonder if there are any feathers in here. A long white one would be just the thing."

"Oh, Jo! Here's some burlap. Perfect for when Audacia disguises herself as a beggar."

Meg threw the burlap over her head and peeked out at Jo.

"Capital! Now we must find something dashing for Teddy, or he'll be disappointed. We do spoil him so," Jo said theatrically, even though she took great pride in her boots and whatever scraps of fabric made her into a duke.

They had been talking so fast and rustling fabric so loudly that they hadn't heard the knock on the door. Suddenly Hannah appeared, wiping her hands on her apron.

"You have a caller, Miss Meg."

"Oh, dear. What is it, Hannah?"

"A Miss . . . hmmm . . . Pomry?"

"Pomeray?" Meg wailed. "Heavens! Oh, Jo, look at the room!"

"I'd take the burlap off my head, if I were you," Jo advised, snatching up as many scraps of material as she could. She tripped over Marmee's footstool and everything in her arms went flying.

"Never mind that, Jo—just go to the kitchen," Meg whispered frantically. "You're wearing knickers and a mustache!"

"Perhaps she'll think me a suitor and try to win me with her charms," Jo said wickedly.

"Go!" Meg urged, giving her sister a not-so-gentle shove. Jo stumbled toward the door to the dining room.

Trying to compose herself, Meg thought of every detail Sallie had told her about Lily Pomeray. Her father was a businessman from New York. Her mother had passed away when Lily was a young child. Beneath her cool facade, the dear girl must long for a good friend, Meg thought.

The gentle sound of a female throat being

cleared caused Meg to freeze for an instant. She composed her features and turned.

Lily Pomeray stood in the doorway. She wore a walking suit of silver gray edged with white velvet. Her raven hair gleamed against a matching white velvet bonnet trimmed with purple silk violets and a wide green satin ribbon that was tied in a jaunty fashion near one ear.

Meg noted all this in a glance. She felt no envy—only feminine interest. She could admire the suit without wishing she could wear it. If she did wear it, she was sure she would feel so queer and grand that she would not be able to leave the house.

Though perhaps she wouldn't mind wearing the bonnet. . . .

Lily's bright glance swept the parlor, lingering on the scraps of fabric and rags thrown on the sofa and trailing on the floor.

"Dear me, I've interrupted your . . . work," she said. "Yes. How dreadful of me. You are Miss March, I presume?"

Meg nodded. "How do you do, Miss Pomeray. Please," she added, clearing off a space on the sofa, "do sit down."

Lily perched on the edge of the sofa. "Please

forgive my presumption, Miss March. But Sallie encouraged me to call upon you. She said that though you are the most proper girl she knows, you do not cling to propriety when a friend is in need. You would not mind my calling."

Meg's brain whirled. She tried not to think of the rag bag upended on the floor, or her disheveled hair. She dropped the burlap she was clutching. She composed her hands in her lap. Clinging desperately to her dignity, she nodded encouragingly at Lily.

"Sallie was quite right," she said warmly. "I'm very glad you called."

"That was your sister I saw withdrawing when I entered?" Lily asked.

Meg nodded. "Josephine. Jo. She—well, we—we were assembling costumes for a . . . family theatrical." In a stealthy movement, she kicked the burlap under Marmee's chair.

"How charming," Lily said.

"How do you find Concord, Miss Pomeray?" Meg asked politely.

"I have fallen in love with Concord, Miss March," Lily said, leaning closer and speaking in a low, thrilling voice. "I must confess, I argued against the move with my father. His business requires so much travel that he was longing for peace during his leisure time. But I was not. I could not imagine leaving the bustle of New York City. I came out last year, you know, and there are so many amusements there! The Academy of Music, and the opera, of course, and driving, and shopping—Well, I didn't see how I would live, how I would simply *survive* in a small city such as Concord. But Miss March, the beauty of it! The simplicity! I adore it."

"I'm happy to hear it," Meg said. "I love Concord, too. Though of course, I've always lived here and have no basis for comparison, as you do."

"You must travel to Boston frequently," Lily observed.

Not as frequently as I would like, Meg longed to say, remembering Sallie's party. "Not very often," she admitted.

"Shall I make a confession, Miss March?" Lily asked. "Yes, I must. Sallie Gardiner wore the most charming gown the other day. It was trimmed in such a cunning fashion. And when I asked who her seamstress could be in a town such as Concord—for it seemed quite French to me, I assure you—she revealed all. Imagine my surprise when I discovered that the dressmaker was merely a friend with exquisite taste! It was you, Miss March."

"I helped Sallie trim a gown," Meg said. "That's all."

"Modesty! One of my most favorite virtues!" Lily laughed. "And one I constantly strive to cultivate in myself. Now. Should I confess something shocking, Miss March? Yes."

Lily leaned forward again. Her bright green eyes, the color of unripe apples, fixed on Meg. Meg was fascinated. Though there was an air of condescension in Lily's manner that she felt unsure of, the girl had charm. There was no denying it. Meg felt herself pulled into the spell of those bright eyes.

"My father has forbidden me to buy clothes in Paris this year," Lily said. She lifted one shoulder in a shrug. "Because of the war. How tiresome!"

Meg felt her cheeks flush. Lily was her guest, and she could not be rude. But she could not let such a remark pass. Imagine thinking of the cost to her wardrobe when men were suffering and dying, and Meg's own father had volunteered to serve?

"I'm sure it must be hard, not to have as many pretty things," Meg said. Under her soft tone was a glint of steel that outsiders rarely saw. "But I can't help but think of our men, who are doing without warm clothes and food, and giving up home and family, perhaps even their lives, to preserve our Union. My father is one of them. I suppose they would find such a sacrifice patriotic."

Lily's gloved hand flew to her mouth. "Dear me, Miss March, I have offended you. It was such a thoughtless remark. I was not thinking . . . of what I should have been thinking. You must forgive me, yes?"

Meg's heart warmed. Lily looked sincerely sorry. And she did not mean to make her guest uncomfortable. Meg impulsively reached out and covered Lily's hand with her own for an instant. "There is nothing to forgive, Miss Pomeray. The war affects us in both deep *and* trivial ways. There are days when the trivial seems terribly important. I have felt that, too."

Lily looked at her wonderingly. "Sallie was right. You are truly kind."

Meg leaned back again. "Now. You were about to reveal a shocking confession, Miss Pomeray?" she asked, smiling.

"Yes, returning to the trivial," Lily said, making a comical face that caused Meg to warm to her. "Gowns. My father will not let me send to Paris for my gowns, and I'm afraid I've run through my allowance for the season. Yet I'm dying for something new. Sallie said you might help me to freshen up my wardrobe."

Meg felt flustered. "Miss Pomeray, I'm not a dressmaker—"

"I know," Lily rushed in. "I realize how much I am asking. You would have my tremendous gratitude, Miss March."

Meg hesitated. She could not refuse a favor to *anyone*—and saying no to Lily Pomeray seemed close to impossible.

"I thought," Lily said, "if I sent my carriage, and you would be so kind, you could look through my wardrobe and suggest any changes you thought appropriate."

Jo would call her a goose, and Marmee would most likely think she was wasting her time, helping a rich young woman with an already lovely wardrobe spend even more time adorning herself.

But Meg didn't care. She could work with beautiful fabrics and colors, and she would be a friend to Lily Pomeray!

"Of course I'll help you, Miss Pomeray," she said.

Lily smiled her gracious smile, revealing small, even teeth. "Please call me Lily," she said. "I feel that we are already friends."

CHAPTER FIVE

Mademoiselle Meg

*M*eg pored over *Le Magasin*. She made sketches and notes. She wanted to be prepared for the grand occasion of advising Lily. Meg even raided Amy's box of pencils and tried out color combinations in the blank pages of her journal.

One quiet evening after supper, Meg scribbled notes to herself in her journal.

> *Narrow green satin sash?*
> *Tulle undersleeve in pink?*

Blue ribbon lacing on back of white muslin over-dress of illusion?—looped with fresh flowers?
Chenille drop buttons!!!

There was no sound in the parlor but the crackle of the fire and the noise of Jo turning a page in her book. Beth was quietly sewing, and Amy was pretending to study, but was spending more time daydreaming. Marmee was hemming a skirt.

Meg scratched away at her journal. Using Amy's pencils, she scratched out an area of sky blue, then put a splotch of blush pink next to it. It was pretty, but perhaps yellow would look prettier. Meg tried the color, then turned to a fresh page and wrote:

Tomorrow Lily carries me away in her carriage to Locust Manor. My nerves are all in a flutter. I want to be helpful, but I fear my sophistication has been overvalued by Sallie. After all, I am not the originator of the ideas! I am merely interpreting the eye of Monsieur Worth, in Paris, and the tales of the stylish women there.

But thinking about satins and silks comforts me, I must own. It reminds me that there is a world out there of ease and luxury, a world in which I could have found a place at one time. It is not that I yearn for riches. I know better. It is the memory of better times that comforts me. And talking of dresses and bonnets instead of poverty and war brings that world back to me.

Foolish I may be. But somehow, I cannot stop myself. I want Lily Pomeray to value my friendship. I want to belong to her inner circle.

How difficult it is, when you want something so much, to stop yourself from wanting it!

Meg's pen dropped, and she gazed into the fire. She did not notice Marmee's eyes on her, or the line of concern between her mother's eyebrows.

Meg sat on a tufted footstool in Lily's dressing room, which was larger than Meg's bedroom. Heaped all around her were ball gowns, walking skirts, everyday dresses, morning dresses, afternoon dresses, and evening dresses—frothy pinks, shimmering greens, bright blues, and deep, luxurious purples and maroons.

Lily sat on a guilt armchair, facing her. Her face was rapt as Meg sorted through the collection, studying beautiful gowns.

"Monsieur Worth doesn't use taffeta, or even moire very much," Meg explained. "Because of him, satins are popular again."

"But my pink satin is so old now," Lily said with a sigh.

"But just think how it would look if we replaced those clasps with jet buttons," Meg said. "And instead of those short sleeves, we could drape lace from the shoulders."

Lily's eyes gleamed. "That sounds heavenly. What else?"

"Your canary yellow satin is lovely," Meg said, tapping her pencil against the notebook on her knee. "If we cover it with illusion, it will look like a cloud. And perhaps some beadwork along the hem, if your seamstress can manage it."

"Perfect," Lily murmured.

"As for the fawn-colored afternoon dress, some fresh black chenille trim shall look neat and elegant. I think perhaps three very narrow velvet ribbons along that flounce shall make all the difference. And the sleeve should be tighter and taper at the wrist."

"Meg, you are a genius!" Lily cried, her eyes shining. Her hands were clasped, and she gave Meg a grateful look. "I don't know how I managed without you at all."

Meg felt herself blush. She smiled at Lily. "Fiddlesticks," she said, embarrassed by Lily's praise. But she felt a deep flush of pleasure as well. She was Lily Pomeray's friend!

"Are you ready for dress rehearsal?" Jo asked Meg that Saturday. "I hope you've learned your lines, Audacia."

"Oh, Jo, I can't," Meg told her. "I have to look for new ribbons with Lily. She asked me especially, because she's so bad at choosing."

Jo frowned. "But we're performing 'Audacia's Escapade' next week, Meg."

"You can go over my lines with me on Sunday afternoon, can't you?" Meg asked, distractedly searching for her gloves.

"It's not the same as a dress rehearsal," Jo said, her brows knit.

"Then can't we hold a dress rehearsal after church tomorrow?" Meg suggested.

"Hang it all, Meg, I've got everybody together, for once," Jo said, exasperated. "Tomorrow afternoon Amy is going sketching with her friend Katy, and

Laurie has an engagement. You promised me you'd be available this afternoon."

Meg pulled on her gloves. "I'm sorry, Jo, truly I am. Your rehearsal simply flew out of my head. And Lily will be here any minute. You can't imagine how important this outing is."

Jo lifted an eyebrow. "I thought you said you were searching for ribbons?"

"Yes, and if the blue gown is to be a success, it must be matched with the right shade of rose," Meg said.

Jo strode forward and took Meg's hands in hers. "Dear, sweet Meg," she cried. "You must stop it right now. I'm afraid for you. *J'ai peur, ma soeur. J'ai tres, tres peur!* Oh, Meg, Meg!"

"Jo, that's terrible French," Meg said, laughing while she tried to pull her hands away. "What do you mean, you featherhead?"

Beth and Amy hurried into the room, hearing the commotion. "What is it, Jo?" Amy asked.

"Is Meg all right?" Beth asked anxiously.

Jo released Meg's hands and struck her breast. "Oh, what are we to do!" she cried theatrically. "We have lost her!" Jo staggered past Amy and Beth and fell on the couch. She dropped her head in her hands. "It has happened at last," she said in a hoarse, croaking voice. "This terrible thing we have feared for so long. Our sister has surrendered. She has become . . . she is now . . ." Jo fixed her tragic eyes on her sisters. ". . . Mademoiselle Meg. She is French!"

Meg, Amy, and Beth let out peals of laughter.

Jo's gray eyes were now twinkling. "Do you think a dose of cod liver oil would cure her?" she asked.

"A double dose," Beth agreed solemnly.

"She should be put to bed immediately," Amy suggested.

"And banned from using French phrases ever again," Jo declared. "Not even, *vive la France!* Or *merci.*"

Still chuckling at her impossible, dramatic sister, Meg heard the sound of a carriage. "There's Lily. I must go." She leaned over and kissed Jo on both cheeks. *"Au revoir!"*

Jo screamed in mock horror and fell back on the sofa. "We have lost our sister to taffeta!" she cried.

"Not taffeta. Ribbons!" Meg corrected her with a smile. Then she hurried from the room.

When the door closed, Amy, Beth, and Jo looked at each other. Slowly, their smiles faded.

"Have we really lost her, Jo?" Amy whispered.

"Of course not," Jo said firmly. But she wished she felt as confident as she sounded.

On Monday Meg received a letter in the mail on thick, elegant notepaper. It looked like an invitation, and her heart pounded as she opened it.

My dear Miss March,

You must take pity on me and cross out any engagements from Friday to Sunday this week, for I will have a household of guests and need you in attendance. A masquerade party is planned for the first evening, and there will be numerous other diversions. I know that without your assistance we shall disgrace ourselves with a deplorable lack of taste and imagination. May I plan on your acceptance?

Yours in affectionate haste,
Lily Pomeray

"Marmee!" Meg cried. "I've been invited to Lily Pomeray's house party! May I go, please?"

Marmee looked up from her desk. "A house party?"

"I heard about it when I saw Sallie Gardiner at church," Meg said, clasping her hands. "I never thought I'd be invited. The girls will dine and sleep for two nights, and on Friday night there's to be a party. Oh, Marmee, please let me go!"

Meg's eyes shone, and her face held a pinkish glow.

"I don't know, Meg," Marmee said slowly. "I know the Pomerays are a good family. Still, I don't know this young woman at all."

"But you've been introduced to her," Meg pointed out. "And I've spent so many afternoons with her. And she's a dear acquaintance of the Gardiners and the Moffats, and oh, Marmee, everybody is going!"

Marmee smiled then. She could not refuse Meg when her heart was set on something. "Then I suppose you must go."

Meg flew to Marmee and hugged her round her neck. "Oh, thank you a thousand times!"

"Once shall be sufficient," Marmee said dryly, picking up her pen again.

"It sounds jolly, Meg," Amy said wistfully. "Oh, I wish I were old enough to go!"

"I wouldn't like to be among a household of strangers," Beth said. "I like to sleep in my own little bed."

"I'd better write Lily immediately to accept," Meg said. "Only five days to get my wardrobe together! I do hope it snows, for I heard there will be a sleighing party on Saturday afternoon. I can wear my new muff."

Jo had been sitting quietly by the fire, a book in her hands, half listening to Meg's plans. Now she looked up. "Saturday afternoon! But you can't, Meg!"

Meg was searching for notepaper at Marmee's desk. "Whyever not, Jo?" she asked distractedly.

"How could you have forgotten?" Jo burst out. "Our production of 'Audacia's Escapade' is on Saturday afternoon! All of the neighborhood children are coming, and we're to stay in character and treat them to tea afterward. And you're playing the lead!"

Beth and Amy were silent. They watched their two older sisters with wide eyes.

Meg looked to her mother for assistance, but

Marmee went to her corner and picked up her work-basket. "You must work this out among yourselves, girls."

Meg swung around in her chair, still holding Lily's invitation. Her face flushed. "Oh, Jo, you know how important this invitation is. Can't something be done?"

Jo set her jaw. "I don't see what."

"It would be easy to postpone the production for a week," Meg pointed out. "The children won't mind."

"Of course they'll mind—they'll be shockingly disappointed," Jo said stubbornly.

"Jo," Meg said steadily, "you know how I'm longing to go."

Jo threw her book down. "Then go," she said shortly. "You're quite right. My little plans are just child's play—"

"Jo! I don't mean that at all! Please don't make so much of this."

"You'd most likely bumble about and forget your lines, for your heart hasn't been in it, anyway," Jo went on stormily. "I must give up playing the duke, which breaks my heart. Laurie shall play him, and I must take on Audacia. Of course, I hate playing the heroine, and Teddy shall make me laugh at the most inappropriate times, but *I* don't want to disappoint the children."

With a scornful look at Meg, Jo strode from the room, leaving her sister with Lily's letter crumpled in her hand.

CHAPTER SIX

Arriving in Style

$\mathcal{J}$o couldn't keep her anger at such a fever pitch for long. She had forgiven Meg by supper, but there was a coolness between the sisters that lasted throughout the week. Though the undercurrent of tension caused Amy to creep around the house, Beth to look wistful, and Marmee to be concerned, the preparation for Meg's departure took up so much of everyone's time that no one could dwell on it.

Marmee, Beth, and Amy helped Meg pack her little trunk with the small bits of finery Meg possessed. Meg did not have time to make over her white gown the way she would like, but she managed to sew a pretty violet satin sash for it. With the addition of narrow satin ribbons in the same color at the hem, Meg pronounced herself satisfied.

"It is not near as grand as Lily's gown, or even Sallie's, but the simple style suits me," Meg said as Marmee packed it carefully. "With some fresh flowers for my hair, I shall want for nothing."

"Laurie promised to send you flowers, the way he does before a party," Amy said. "Shall I hint that violets would be the perfect flower?"

"I'm sure whatever Laurie chooses shall be the freshest and most exquisite he can find, but violets *would* be perfect," Meg said, eyeing her new sash.

"It's a pity that he can't accompany you, Meg," Amy said. "You would have a fine time together."

"But Laurie must accompany his uncle to Boston," Beth said wistfully.

"Our young Mr. Laurence values family responsibilities over social commitments," Marmee said.

Meg froze in her tracks. Was Marmee hinting that she was fleeing her family obligations? She wanted to be in Jo's play, but why couldn't anyone understand the importance of one's place in society?

"Where's Jo?" Beth asked anxiously. "It's almost time for you to leave."

Meg pretended to be busy searching for her gloves. "I'm sure I don't know," she said.

The rest of her family fell silent. Amy busied herself with smoothing Meg's handkerchiefs. Marmee adjusted Meg's collar with a soft smile, and Beth went to the window to look out.

"She's probably up in the garret, lost in a book," Meg said with a too-bright smile. "Give her my love, will you?"

"Here's Laurie's carriage, right on time." Beth called from the window. "You'll arrive in style, Meg."

Meg pressed a hand to her beating heart. "How do I look?" she asked.

Marmee smiled. "Like an angel."

"Like a vision," Amy pronounced.

Beth hugged her. "Like our Meg, only ten times prettier."

Hannah led the coachman upstairs for the trunk, and the girls hurried downstairs. Meg tied her bonnet strings the way Lily did, high on the side near one ear. Then she hugged and kissed her sisters and Marmee.

"Remember every single detail," Amy told her. "I *crave* them."

Meg looked at the stairs anxiously. Why wouldn't Jo come? She didn't feel right, leaving without kissing her sister good-bye. Jo's absence proved that she was a good deal angrier at Meg than she had let on.

Marmee saw Meg's anxious look. On the pretense of adjusting the bow on her bonnet, Marmee whispered, "You know that in her heart she wishes you well, dear."

Meg would have to be content with that. She squeezed Marmee's hand.

"Well, I'm ready," she said. She heard the door behind her. It must be the coachman, entering again to hurry her along. "Wish me—"

"Luck!" Jo cried, bounding into the hall, her bonnet askew. "And lace," she said, making a deep bow and handing Meg a parcel wrapped in delicate paper.

"What's this?" Meg asked wonderingly. Her eyes searched Jo's merry face.

"After numerous hints, deep sighs, and veiled suggestions on my part all week long—don't worry, Marmee, I was a model of submission—Aunt March suddenly came to the conclusion that a March girl should not attend an elegant house party without fine lace," Jo said breathlessly. "So, she lent this to you."

Meg unwrapped the parcel. In it was a beautiful length of fine lace. She ran a hand over it in admiration. "Aunt March's Brussels lace!" she breathed. "Oh, how lovely!"

"It's just the thing for your white gown, Meg," Amy said, admiring it. "You can throw it round your shoulders."

"And fasten it with Marmee's garnet brooch," Meg said excitedly. "Oh, Jo!"

She threw herself at her sister and hugged her tightly. "You are the best sister. And I'm so sorry about—"

"It's all right," Jo said, kissing Meg's soft cheek affectionately. "We'll manage without you somehow. Just dazzle that silly set, and I'll be content, dearest Meg."

Meg sat back against the maroon upholstery of the Laurence carriage. The creak of the leather— even the squeak of the wheels—sounded luxurious to her. She was going to a fine party in a fine carriage, and the weather had turned cold enough for her new traveling coat and muff. Meg could not be more content.

The carriage made the turn into Locust Manor's entrance. There was an imposing brick mansion with a wide green lawn dotted with the trees that gave it its name. Meg made sure her gloves were buttoned and her bonnet straight as they trotted up to the front door.

The coachman, Boggs, swung down. His face was a mask of politeness as he opened the door, but his eyes twinkled as he held out an arm to help Meg down the step. Meg and Jo had once borrowed a whip from him to do a proper scene in one of Jo's plays, and he had harbored a soft spot for the girls ever since.

"Thank you, Boggs," Meg whispered under her breath. "Wish me luck."

"The best of it, miss," Boggs replied. "I'll be getting your trunk down."

The massive oak doors opened, and a butler appeared.

"Miss Meg March," Meg said, trying not to sound timid.

A small, confused frown crossed the butler's face. Then he turned to Boggs.

"Please drive round to the side entrance," he told him.

Boggs tipped his hat. He raised his eyebrows at Meg, but helped her back into the carriage and climbed up again.

With a clatter of hooves, they went round the drive and took a narrow path toward the stables and kitchen. Boggs drew up at a smaller door.

A housekeeper came out, wiping her hands on her apron. "Miss March?"

"Yes," Meg called out the window.

"Well, come along then," the housekeeper said.

Again, Boggs handed her down. He swung her trunk on his shoulders and left it outside the door.

"I'll be back for you on Sunday afternoon, Miss March," he told Meg.

Meg watched him go with a feeling of dismay. Would his be the last friendly, familiar face she would see for days?

Don't be a goose, Meg, she scolded herself silently as she followed the housekeeper into a small, cramped foyer. The room was crammed with boots and umbrellas and several large rubber mackintoshes.

"I'll have Grady bring your trunk up," the house-keeper said. "My name is Hill. If you have any problems, you come to me, mind. Don't go bothering Miss Pomeray."

"I shan't," Meg said, surprised at the housekeeper's brusque manner. She had expected to be welcomed by Lily and her father. She had expected to be ushered into the family parlor. She had expected warm smiles. Instead, she was following a house-keeper through a narrow passageway and dodging a bushel of onions.

"Mind your head," the housekeeper said as they passed through a low doorway.

Meg followed Hill up a narrow stairway. They seemed to climb forever. At last, Hill turned down a hall and led her to a door.

"Your room, Miss March," she said, swinging open the door.

Meg stepped inside expectantly. But instead of a grand room with tapestries and velvet curtains, as she'd imagined, this chamber was smaller than her room at home. There was a plain bed and dresser, and a simple white coverlet on the bed.

"It's very nice," Meg murmured. Perhaps the

house was so full that she had been given one of
the smaller rooms.

But at least she was here! And the view out
her window was fine. Although she overlooked the
stables, beyond them she could see a wooded hill
and what Jo would consider a romantic ruined stone
cottage in the distance.

"Miss Pomeray instructed me to say that the
attic trunks will be open for your perusal, Miss
March," Hill said, smoothing a pillow and laying
out a linen towel. "The housemaid, Bridget, will be
bringing along sewing materials and such. Tea will
be served in the kitchen at five, after the guests have
been served."

Meg's knees suddenly felt weak. *After the guests
have been served?*

"And Miss Lily will summon you sometime this
afternoon to outline your duties," Hill said. She gave
a last satisfied look around the small chamber. "Now
I have my duties to attend to."

The door closed behind Hill with a sharp *click*.
Tea in the kitchen?
Outline her duties?
Meg's legs gave way completely, and she sank
onto the hard, narrow bed.

The words clicked into place in her head like puzzle pieces, and the scene suddenly became clear to Meg.

She hadn't been invited to Lily's house party as a guest. She'd been *hired* to be here—as a servant!

CHAPTER SEVEN

Tattered Dignity

*M*eg's first emotion was overwhelming shame. She felt the blood rush to her face. Then, just as quickly, it drained away, making her feel cold and dizzy.

She rose, then sat down again. She wanted to grab her things and run home as fast as she could. But Boggs was most likely long gone.

I could send a note, asking him to return as quickly as possible, Meg thought, standing up again.

She sat. She needed to think this through. Perhaps it was all a misunderstanding. Perhaps any moment now Lily would arrive, her earrings tinkling, her curls swaying, and apologies would tumble from her lips. She would personally escort Meg to another bedroom and make sure she had every comfort. . . .

But the house was silent.

Meg reached into her small bag and removed Lily's letter. She smoothed out the creases and scanned it anxiously.

I will have a household of guests and need you in attendance . . .

I know that without your assistance we shall disgrace ourselves with a deplorable lack of taste and imagination . . .

May I plan on your acceptance?

Slowly, Meg crumpled the letter in her fist. She realized that nowhere in the letter had Lily made it clear she was a guest. As a matter of fact, it did sound as though Lily had hired her to help with the guests' costumes.

Meg rose and paced the small room. "What am I going to do?" she fretted.

The thought of facing the guests filled her with shame. Why, Sallie was here, and Amelia Reston! Friends she had called on, girls she had known since she was small. They would see her here, acting as a servant to Lily Pomeray!

How could she bear such humiliation?

If there was one thing Meg sought to cultivate, it was dignity. The kind of sweet dignity that Marmee had, the kind that told the world that no matter how poor she was, she was worthy of respect. That no matter what life gave her, she would face it bravely and with grace.

But how, Meg thought in despair, could she cling to her dignity in this cold, grand house as a *servant?*

Meg crossed to the window. She pressed her hot forehead against the cold pane. Below her, several stable boys were busy polishing two large sleighs, and one was currying a horse. Though it was a cold day, their jackets were off, for they were working hard and the exertion kept them warm.

Watching them, Meg felt suddenly calmer.

"I must remember that there is no shame attached to being paid a wage for a service well rendered," she said aloud.

How she wished Marmee were there! Her mother could help her, show her the right way to behave.

Meg reached into her soft bag for the journal she had tucked inside at the last minute. She had imagined that she would record the gay happenings here for Amy's sake, as well as her own, for Meg hadn't wanted to forget one detail.

She sat at a small table and began to write.

I must find the courage to face this. I must hold up my head and do my duty. What that duty is, I am not sure. Jo would advise me to leave. But perhaps Marmee would say that I accepted the invitation, and must see it through. For I was the one to misunderstand Lily's request, and by my acceptance, I made a promise to help her.

Perhaps this will teach me a lesson about my pride. It shall be very hard, but the best lessons always are, are they not?

I must remind myself that everyone knows I am poor. Everyone knows that I earn my own bread. I am a governess, not a fine lady. I have never felt ashamed of that. Father and Mother wouldn't want me to be. So if Lily asked me here to help her then help her I must. No matter what it costs me.

A knock sounded, and the housekeeper entered.

"Here's your trunk," she announced, as a young man dropped it on the floor with a crash. The housekeeper winced. "Grady!" She cuffed the boy on the ear. "You're to *place* the trunk on the floor, not go throwing it down like a hay bale!"

"Sorry, ma'am."

"Get along with you, then," Hill said, frowning. She turned back to Meg. "Miss Lily will see you now, Miss March. Follow along."

Meg closed her journal and tucked it back into her bag. She straightened her skirts and her shoulders. Gathering her courage—and her tattered dignity—she left the servant's wing and followed Hill to the grand chambers of the manor house.

CHAPTER EIGHT

Promises to Keep

*H*ill ushered Meg into Lily's lavishly furnished private sitting room. Lily was sitting on a pink satin loveseat, and she rose as Meg entered.

"Meg!" she cried with the same friendliness. "You're here at last. May I say at the outset that your accommodations are not what I'd wish? But as you know, the house is full. When we had the house in Rhinebeck, we could easily accommodate twenty guests, but we are a bit cramped here in the manor, I fear."

"My room is quite comfortable, thank you," Meg said politely.

Lily twirled in front of her. "Have you not noticed my gown? I trimmed it in spring green, just as you suggested. And the ribbon matches perfectly, don't you agree? How I admire your taste! Please do sit, Meg, for we have heaps to discuss."

Meg perched on the edge of the loveseat. Lily sat next to her and half turned to face her.

"I'm so thrilled you accepted my invitation, for I was in a flutter about the masquerade for days," Lily said. "Then I had an inspiration. Meg shall help me!"

"What exactly will happen tonight?" Meg asked.

"It shall be such fun," Lily said, her green eyes glinting. "After supper, the guests shall withdraw to the library, where a silver bowl will be filled with slips of paper. On each slip of paper will be written a name. I've chosen a mythological theme, so each guest will get a name of a figure from Greek mythology. The women will have pink slips, and the men blue—aren't I clever? And for the grand prize for the most imaginative costume, the winner will receive the silver bowl! I'm sure Concord has never seen such an extravaganza. It shall be talked about all season!"

"I'm sure," Meg murmured. "But how shall the guests assemble their costumes?"

"Oh, I forgot the most important part!" Lily said merrily. "How silly of me. Well, the trunks will be brought downstairs. The guests will have the run of the trunks—the ladies in the drawing room, and the gentlemen in the billiard room. They may also ask the servants for help and prowl about the grounds. They will have two hours to assemble a costume. And then there will be dancing, and the prize will be awarded at the end of the evening. It shall be such fun!"

As Lily chattered, Meg struggled with her feelings. She knew that she must follow through on her promise, as she'd decided earlier. She would do it as quietly as possible. Perhaps Lily would have her assemble the materials beforehand, and she would not have to face the guests at all.

"Shall I be in the drawing room, then?" Meg asked cautiously. "To assist the ladies?"

Lily waved a hand. "Oh, I haven't worked out the details yet. I'll send for you, or send a note to your room, telling you what's expected." In a subtle show of nerves, she played with a ring on her finger. "As for the issue of payment . . ." she said, her voice trailing off.

Meg stiffened. She should have expected that this conversation would take place. Of course Lily planned to pay her!

"I haven't said anything before, Meg. It's so much jollier if such things aren't mentioned. And we're friends, as well as . . . well, employer and employee, I suppose. I don't like to put on airs."

Yes, I thought we were friends, Meg cried silently. *But friends do not pay friends for favors!*

"Your situation is so delicate, you see," Lily said. "Your family had come upon hard times, and depends upon charity—"

"You're mistaken," Meg interrupted coolly. "We are not destitute, Miss Pomeray. We work for our bread honestly."

"Oh, please go on calling me Lily," Lily said in a rush. "I do so want things to be easy and natural between us. Now, I suppose you've been keeping some sort of account for me. And I assure you, I shall pay handsomely for the service you'll render me over the next few days. An envelope will be waiting for you when you leave on Sunday." She sat back with a sigh. "There, that's done. I do so hate to speak of such things, don't you?"

"There's no need to speak of them at all," Meg said, as smoothly as she could. "I'm afraid there has been a misunderstanding, Miss . . . Lily. I cannot possibly accept payment. I came here as a personal favor to you. Any advice I have given has been on that basis."

Now Lily looked surprised. "But Meg—your family. You cannot afford to—"

"That is for me to decide," Meg said firmly. "When it comes to charity, one cannot ever be too rich or too poor to offer a helping hand. Don't you agree?"

Two spots of color appeared on Lily's white cheeks. The reference to charity had angered her. Meg hadn't meant to imply that her service to Lily was a charity. She wished she could snatch back the words, for they sounded unkind.

"Perhaps I expressed myself badly," Meg added. "What I meant to say is that my position is firm. Accept my help and advice on the basis of friendship. Nothing more—or less."

Lily pressed her lips together in a thin line. "Well now. I see I must accept. I suppose I owe you a debt." She looked extremely displeased at the thought.

Meg stood. "Not at all," she said as warmly as she could.

She waited for Lily to make an answering comment, but Lily remained silent. Her lips were still tight, as though she were afraid of what she would say if she spoke. Puzzled, Meg gave a short nod and withdrew.

CHAPTER NINE

The Dangers of Mazes

*M*eg longed for a good "ramble," as Jo would say. The wind would cool her hot cheeks, and the exercise would calm her mind. It was almost teatime. No doubt the guests would be gathering in one of the formal rooms. She would have the woods and lawns to herself.

Meg quickly dressed in her outdoor things and ran down the back staircase. She hurried past the stables and found a path that wound through a wood and up the hill past the ruined stone cottage. Clouds bumped into each other and rolled overhead, and the sun kept her warm from the chill breeze. She felt better, just being able to tramp about.

For her return, Meg decided to take an interesting-looking path that snaked off in another direction. It brought her to a side lawn on the opposite side of the manor house. Ahead Meg saw tall hedges in a boxlike shape. There was a break in the hedge, and Meg went closer to investigate. Peering inside the gap, she saw a small path that went a few feet, then abruptly turned a corner.

"Why, it's a maze," she murmured to herself. "What fun!"

Meg had never seen an outdoor maze, though Laurie had told her of a "ripping devil of a one" that he'd investigated in England. She walked down the grassy path, made false turns, doubled back again, smiling at her own folly. She could not seem to choose the correct path, no matter how long she tried to puzzle out her direction. *How my sisters would enjoy it!* she thought.

She reached the middle and was rewarded by a statue of Artemis, the goddess of the hunt. A small stone bench invited rest. Meg sank gratefully onto it. She wished Amy were there to sketch the statue and the hedge, which was clipped into the shapes of various animals.

The exercise and the maze had driven her troubles from her mind. But suddenly Meg heard voices. She could not tell where they were coming from, but she knew they were near. Then she heard the sound of Lily's high, trilling laugh.

Meg froze for an instant. Was she intruding on a place where she shouldn't be? Her position at the manor was so strange. She wasn't quite a servant, but she certainly wasn't a guest, free to wander at will. Oh, why hadn't she stayed toward the rear of the house!

Meg rose and quickly left the small clearing, but in her confusion could not remember which path to take. She struck out to the right, hurrying down the grassy path.

But she seemed to be going *toward* the voices rather than away from them. Meg stopped. Should she turn back?

The voices grew louder, and Meg realized that they were on the other side of the hedge.

Then she heard her name.

"The Marches are an old Concord family, Lily,"

a voice said. It was Sallie. "It is only lately that they have fallen on hard times."

"Still, for the girl to tell me that helping me was *charity* on her part! I never was so insulted!"

Her cheeks burning, Meg hurried down the path. It was not polite to eavesdrop on a private conversation. One seldom heard good news, in fact. So she had offended Lily earlier. She hadn't meant to, and she'd tried to set it right. The girl seemed determined to be insulted.

Meg sped around a corner. Then she ran down the path and turned right. She ended up exactly where she'd been! The maze was so confusing. She didn't know where to turn next, and she did not want to meet Lily and Sallie face-to-face.

". . . but they are dreadfully poor, are they not?" Lily was saying. "And as a newcomer I must be especially careful. Miss March is a governess, and that untidy sister is a paid companion. Surely they don't move in the first circles."

"Well, perhaps not the *first*, anymore," Sallie murmured. "But—"

"And you, dear Sallie, must see that a girl simply must be careful about her place in society. I would advise you to keep your distance, especially since you're now such a dear friend of mine. But you aren't a particular friend of Miss March's, are you?"

Meg waited, her cheeks burning. Surely Sallie would now proclaim her friendship. Surely her good friend would show Lily Pomeray that snobbery had no place in a good heart.

"Not a very particular friend," Sallie answered faintly after a pause.

Meg's eyes filled with tears. She could bear anything—but not Sallie's betrayal. Her eyes stung, and she blundered down the path. She didn't care if she made a wrong turn. She had to escape this maze! She had to return to her quiet room.

Blindly she ran down one path after another. In her haste she lost all sense of direction. At last she wheeled round a corner—and almost ran into Lily and Sallie.

"Pardon me," Meg said in a choked voice, tears standing in her eyes. She could not look at Lily, and she had only a confused sense of Sallie's guilty face.

"Miss March," Lily said serenely. "I did not know you were about the grounds."

"Yes, pardon me, please, good day." Meg jumbled the words together in a rush and hurried past them toward the safety of her quiet room.

CHAPTER TEN

Old Lace and New Society

*T*he brusque housekeeper, Hill, turned out to have a softer side. When Meg rushed through the kitchen, Hill must have noted the trace of tears on Meg's face. She accepted Meg's explanation of a headache and kindly offered to bring Meg's tea to her room.

So Meg had a few precious minutes to compose herself. First, she cried her fill. Then, she drew herself together and splashed water on her face. By the time tea arrived, she felt calm.

"These came for you," Hill said, placing a box on Meg's table. "And there's a note from Miss Lily on the tray."

"Thank you, Hill," Meg said. Leaving Lily's note for now, she hurried to open the box. Nestled in tissue were two exquisite bouquets of violets.

Meg picked up the card tucked among the blooms.

FOR MADEMOISELLE MEG, THE BELLE OF ANY BALL.
REGARDS, THEODORE LAURENCE.
P.S. JO SENDS A MESSAGE—BON CHANCE!

Bon chance meant "good luck" in French. It was Jo's way of telling Meg that she would support her sister, even if Meg yearned to be a fine "mademoiselle." *If only Jo could see me now!* Meg thought wryly.

She touched the flowers, smiling. Leave it to Laurie and Jo to cheer her up.

She poured her tea, then sat down to read Lily's note.

My dear Miss March,

"Ah," Meg said aloud, "so I am now Miss March again!"

Will you do me the kindness of waiting in the morning room while the guests are dining? I will direct that your dinner be served to you there. I shall come to you as soon as the names are drawn for the masquerade.

Hill will conduct you promptly at seven.

Lily Pomeray

The note was so formal! So different from Lily's usual manner. Obviously she had not yet forgiven Meg.

This was turning out to be quite a trial on her spirits. Once again she wished her sisters were nearby. Her journal was becoming an impassioned mix of hurt feelings and logic, anger and hope.

I cannot expect Lily to treat me as a friend. Our time together has been short. But I cannot help feeling hurt and angry at Sallie, even while I understand her. She wants Lily as a friend so badly! Once I felt as she did. Why is it that we tend to run after those who don't care about us? For I suspect that Sallie's friend-ship hardly means to Lily what it means to Sallie.

But perhaps I am being unfair. Time will tell. Now, I must compose myself and remember to act with kindness when next I meet Sallie. Marmee would want me to do so. And even though Jo might storm about and talk of giving Sallie a good thrashing—and it makes me smile to think of it—I know that Jo, too, would control her temper and be as kind to Sallie as she could. It is always better to act with our better natures, no matter what trials we bear.

Meg closed the journal with a sigh. The tiny clock on the modest bedside table told her that it was time to dress. She tried not to feel sad as she stepped into the white gown she had packed with such eagerness. When she took out Aunt March's lace, she smiled. Jo's love and support was as strong as a beating heart.

It gave her strength to drape the fine lace around her shoulders and fasten it with Marmee's garnet brooch. She tucked the violets into her sash and wound a few blooms in her curls.

"Well," she told her reflection, "I may not have

been invited to the ball. But at least 1 am dressed for it!"

Meg barely touched her supper. A fire had been lit in the morning room, but it seemed a gloomy, formal place. It was most likely more cheerful when flooded with sunlight in the mornings. Meg drew her chair closer to the cheerful blaze.

Several trunks sat on the carpet. Meg had sifted through the items. There were lovely bolts of fabric, ribbons, rolls of colored paper, thick leather belts, tunics, and a set of filmy curtains. Strings of beads and a jumble of piano shawls. Relics of old parties, old rooms.

A butler appeared and whisked away her tray. Every so often a burst of laughter would reach Meg's ears, even though the dining room was down the hall and both doors were closed. It must be a merry party. Meg couldn't help feeling lonely in the gloomy room.

But then she fingered her lace and pressed her fingers against Marmee's brooch. She thought of how Amy would tell her how nice she looked, and imagined Jo saying, "Bear up, dear Meg!" And Beth would approve of her reluctance to break a promise.

Meg heard the sound of footsteps in the hall. High voices and laughter came to her. The ladies were withdrawing to the drawing room, then. Soon the men would join them, and the masquerade game would begin.

After a few minutes had passed, Meg heard the sound of the door opening behind her. It must be Lily, coming to see how she was faring.

Meg rose and turned. A handsome young man stood in the doorway, dressed in evening clothes.

Startled, both of them said nothing for a moment. Then they spoke at the same time.

"Excuse me—"

They smiled.

"I'm sorry to intrude," the young man said. He bowed and began to withdraw.

"It's no intrusion," Meg said quickly. "I should be the one to leave." After all, he was a guest. If he wanted to use the morning room, she should be the one to leave. Lily could send for her upstairs.

She moved toward the door. "I will return upstairs," she murmured.

"Why?" the young man said. "I mean—oh, jiminy, I've been saying everything wrong, all night long. Please do stay, would you? I don't want you to leave on my account."

Meg couldn't help smiling. His earnest concern and frank nature reminded her of Laurie.

"What I mean is," he went on, his blue eyes dancing, "it appears I'm not the only one longing for escape."

"Escape?" Meg asked. "Escape from what?"

"From the exhausting burden of being clever, I'm afraid," he said, making a comical face that made Meg smile. "For I'm not clever at all, and supper was a grim affair for me."

"I see," Meg said thoughtfully. "As I don't know you, I shall have to take your word for your lack of cleverness."

"Oh, dear," he said, frowning. "Don't do that. I would much rather you take me for far cleverer than I am."

"Now I am quite confused," Meg said. "I don't know if I will take you any way at all."

They laughed. Meg was surprised to find herself feeling comfortable with him, even though she rarely felt at ease with strange men. But he was so comical and grave at the same time that she couldn't help warming to him.

"Permit me to introduce myself," he said "My name is Andrew Goodchurch."

"Margaret March," Meg answered.

He held out his hand, and Meg hesitated.

"Oh, bother, shaking hands isn't quite the thing, is it," Andrew said, snatching back his hand. "I suppose I should bow, or something. Now don't smile— I told you that I wasn't clever."

"I suspect that you are a great deal too clever for your own good," Meg said lightly.

"Since I've already been horribly rude, I shall risk an impertinent question," Andrew said, taking a few steps into the room and standing by Meg. "Why have *you* retreated to an empty room? Are you hiding, as I am?"

"Not at all," Meg said. "I am here at Miss Pomeray's request."

"I see. But why aren't you at dinner? Are you feeling poorly? For you look remarkably well."

As Andrew Goodchurch heard his own words, he blushed a deep red. Meg rather liked his shyness, for she did not know how to interpret his remark. If anyone else had complimented her on such short acquaintance, she would have thought him improper.

"I am not a guest," Meg said quickly. "I'm an acquaintance of Miss Pomeray, and she asked my help with the masquerade."

"An acquaintance, but not a guest," Andrew said, frowning. "That is very odd, I must say."

Meg didn't know how to respond to that. How could she explain her situation when she hardly understood it herself?

But Meg was saved from having to respond when the door opened, and Lily Pomeray walked in.

CHAPTER ELEVEN

Meg Takes a Stand

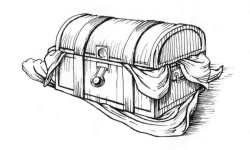

*F*or perhaps the first time since she'd met Lily, Meg saw the young woman sincerely flustered. Both hands gripped her delicate fan, and her laugh was like shattering crystal.

"I declare, here is my runaway," she said to Andrew. "Mr. Goodchurch, you are trying to the patience of your hostess. The game is about to begin."

Andrew bowed. "I beg your pardon, Miss Pomeray. I stumbled into this room, and Miss March was kind enough to allow me to stay."

Lily arched her brow. "Yes, Miss March is known for her kindness."

"I'm sure it is only one among many virtues," Andrew said, with an admiring glance at Meg.

Lily's pale face flushed a deep, angry red. Her glance at Meg was furious. She opened her fan with a *snap* and fanned herself.

"Mr. Goodchurch, would you be so kind as to join the ladies?" she asked. "I need a word with Miss March."

"Certainly." But Andrew hesitated. "Shall I see you again, Miss March?"

"Mr. Goodchurch?" Lily's polite tone edged into a squeak.

Meg could see that Andrew was puzzled as to Lily's manner. But a gentleman did not refuse his hostess.

"Good evening," he said with a bow, and walked out.

As soon as the door closed behind him, Lily turned to Meg. "I'll thank you not to engage the guests in conversation." She pursed her lips in a most unappealing way, adding, "One would think that the attention of *one* admirer would be quite enough, Miss March."

"One admirer?" Meg was confused.

"I saw Mr. Laurence's flowers arrive," Lily said.

Laurie? Meg would have laughed aloud if Lily had given her the chance.

"Mr. Goodchurch is a guest here," Lily stated firmly. "You would be well advised to remember that, Miss March."

Meg inclined her head. She would not apologize to Lily for simple courtesy. It was not her fault that Andrew Goodchurch had appeared.

Lily snapped her fan closed. Tossing her head, she hurried out the door after Andrew.

Meg sat by the fire again to compose herself. There were only a few hours left of the evening, she told herself. Once she had assembled the costumes, she could go to bed.

Lily returned in a few minutes. Closing the door quietly behind her, she hurried toward Meg.

"Daphne!" she announced as she crossed the room. "That was the name I picked. I so wanted to choose Helen of Troy! Well, it can't be helped. Have you any ideas?"

"Daphne was a wood nymph and a hunter," Meg said, trying to remember her mythology.

"Yes, yes, I know that," Lily snapped.

"So to start with, we'll need a bow and arrow of some kind—"

"I'm sure there is one in the nursery," Lily said, brightening. "There are all sorts of toys up there, for when my sister's children come to stay."

"I could cover it in green paper," Meg said. She frowned, thinking. "Daphne was changed into a laurel tree by her father to protect her from Apollo. I know what we can do! We can make a costume showing you halfway through the transformation. We'll need leaves, and perhaps some bark. . . ."

Lily nodded slowly. "That sounds capital. I'll win the prize for certain."

"Let me see if I can find something in these trunks for you," Meg said. She sifted through the fabrics and objects. "It will be good for you to have a sash, or a bodice of some kind, in the colors of the forest. Something a hunter might wear." She drew out a russet fabric. "This might work," she mused. "We'll need a belt. . . ."

Suddenly a thought occurred to her. She looked up at Lily. "But where are the other guests?" Meg asked. "These items should be shared. Aren't I to help them as well?"

"Oh, you don't have to do that," Lily said, waving her hand. "I am the hostess, so I think it fair if I alone have the benefit of your advice. I arranged to bring some items here, to this room, while the guests have the run of the trunks in the drawing room. They have plenty of things to choose from. I do so long to win the prize! I *must* win it!"

Meg dropped the russet cloth and rose to her feet. "Do you mean to tell me that you will shut me away here, and no one will know that someone helped you?"

"Why should they have to know?" Lily asked, picking up the russet cloth and smoothing it over her shoulder.

"And the guests must fashion their costumes on their own?" Meg persisted.

"I directed the servants to fetch anything they might request," Lily said. "Do you really feel the russet cloth is best? I look so much better in green—"

"Miss Pomeray," Meg interrupted sternly. "I fear that what you're suggesting is not fair to the others. It is, in fact, cheating."

Lily's eyes blazed. "How dare you accuse me of cheating!" she cried shrilly.

Meg remained as steady as she could. "I only point out what I think is fair."

"Well, it doesn't matter what you think is fair," Lily said. "It only matters what I think."

Meg was speechless for a moment. She could not believe that she had once yearned for this girl's friendship. She had been blinded by her charm, her grace—and yes—her social position. She had imagined the generous heart that must beat beneath those fine silks. But Lily was vain and selfish. She did not deserve Meg's friendship.

Marmee's voice suddenly rose in Meg's mind. She remembered Amy weeping over a slight she had suffered at school.

You must remember, Amy, that the selfish, cruel people in the world are often lonely and afraid. If you meet them with love, not match their cruelty, you will not only feel better about your conduct, you will make your relations smoother.

Perhaps Lily did not have the love in her home that Meg did. There was something feverish about her attempt to capture Sallie's friendship, to control Andrew's behavior, to win the silver bowl. Was it because she needed those things to feel loved and wanted?

At any rate, it would take only a little effort to

mix kindness with firmness. So it was with a gentle hand that Meg leaned over and closed the trunk.

"It matters to me what I think," she said. "I shan't help you, Miss Pomeray. Not unless I can help the others as well."

"But you must!" Lily cried angrily.

Meg placed a hand on Marmee's garnet brooch. It felt as warm as her mother's touch.

"I cannot," Meg answered softly.

CHAPTER TWELVE

Parlor Games

*M*eg saw that Lily was furious. Her hand clutched the russet fabric to her body, and her apple-green eyes blazed.

"I suppose I am forced to agree," Lily said icily. "Shall I summon the ladies, then? Is that your *direction?*"

"Merely my request," Meg said.

Lily wheeled about and stalked from the room. Moments later, the morning room was crowded with guests. The lids of the trunks were flung open, and scarves, fabric, beads, and hats were strewn on the carpet. Laughing young women wound fabric into turbans, curtains into capes, and scarves into sashes.

Meg flew from girl to girl, advising, pinning, and sewing. She twisted ivy into wreaths and fashioned belts out of brightly colored paper. She found an old box and filled it with paper snakes for "Pandora" to carry.

"Miss March, you are a marvel," Cora Goodchurch told her. She had drawn the name Demeter, goddess of the harvest. She touched her headdress made of fruit and woven grasses. "How did you contrive such a thing? I do hope I won't trip and cause it to fall."

"Then the rest of the guests shall have dessert," Meg said gaily. "Those pears are ripe, I daresay."

Cora laughed heartily, and Meg joined in. She was enjoying herself far more than she expected. She hadn't realized how well making costumes for the March girls' theatricals had prepared her for this task. *Leave it to a March to make merry play out of odds and ends,* Meg thought, still smiling at Cora.

"Oh, Miss March! Miss March!" Another guest, Maude Higbie, called for her.

Meg hurried over. Maude had her hands full of

various items: a man's black silk hat, a yellow piano shawl, and a small rug. Meg couldn't help smiling at the jumble.

"I've drawn Iris, and I don't know what to do," Maude said. "Time has almost run out! You are so clever. Can you help me?"

"Of course I shall," Meg said soothingly. "I know just the thing. Wait just a moment."

Meg ran to the third trunk, which held an assortment of silk scarves. She filled her hands with various colors, then hurried back to Maude.

"I have just enough time to quickly baste these together," she told her. "Aren't they lovely?"

"But what shall I do with them?" Maude asked, puzzled.

"Look," Meg said, spreading them out on her lap. "Red, orange, yellow, green, blue, violet—the colors of the rainbow. That's the symbol for Iris. We'll make a long sash from one shoulder, round your waist, and let it flutter behind you. And perhaps if you'll take these scarves and twist them together, we can tie them round your forehead."

"Perfect!' Maude cried. "I shall be splendid!"

It didn't take Meg long to finish the stitches, then pin the sash on Maude's pretty white gown.

Then she tied the twisted rope around Maude's forehead and knotted it in back.

As she worked, Meg peeked over Maude's shoulder. Sallie Gardiner stood apart from the girls, twisting her slip of paper in her lap. She was not laughing, or trying on a headdress, or standing on tiptoe to peek into the mirror, like the other girls. She looked miserable, Meg noted with a pang.

She walked over. "Sallie? Can I help you in any way?"

Sallie looked at her. Guilt marked her face, and she bit her lip. "No, thank you, Meg, I shall manage. I don't want to trouble you."

"It's no trouble," Meg said warmly. "I am here to assist you, so as Jo would say, 'Command me!' Now, which goddess did you pick?"

"Hestia," Sallie told her. "Goddess of the hearth. I don't have a single idea, Meg. Shall I carry a coal scuttle about?"

Meg smiled. "I think we can do better than that. There's a lovely flame-colored silk shawl in one of the trunks. I don't think any of the girls has claimed it. Perhaps we can wind that about you. Then . . . perhaps if you carry a candle, that will symbolize fire. And I will make you a headdress, too, of yellow paper."

"Will you, Meg? I didn't like to ask. And I'm sure I don't deserve it." Sallie ended in a whisper, and her eyes darted toward Lily.

"Don't talk such nonsense. Come, we must hurry," Meg directed.

She wound the cloth about Sallie and found a narrow taperstick with a gold candle for her to carry. Then, she made a crown out of canary paper and ivy.

Meg stepped back to judge the result. "Very proper, I think," she told Sallie. "It does need a final touch, however."

Meg unclasped Marmee's garnet brooch. "A piece of liquid fire would do nicely to fasten the cloth against your gown," she said.

"Not your mother's brooch!" Sallie cried.

"I know that it is in good hands," Meg assured her, pinning the brooch to Sallie's shoulder.

"Now your lace will fall off your shoulders," Sallie said.

"I shall just tie it, like this," Meg said, demonstrating. "I must be very careful, for it's only borrowed from Aunt March, and she treasures it."

Lily had drawn closer to the two girls. Meg had spent the most time on Lily's costume, and she looked every inch a Greek goddess, with ivy trailing down her skirt and crowning her shining dark hair. Meg had even pinned bits of bark and leaves to her sash, to symbolize her transformation into a laurel tree. She carried a bow that Meg had wrapped in emerald green paper.

Lily eyed the lace around Meg's white shoulders. "That lace would go so well with my costume," she said.

In that instance, Meg knew that Lily had only made the suggestion because she knew how much Meg treasured the lace. But she quickly unknotted it.

"You must take it, then," she said quietly.

"It doesn't suit your costume at all, Lily," Sallie spoke up. "It will only look silly."

"I don't agree," Lily replied coolly, taking the lace from Meg's hands.

Just then there was a knock at the morning room door. Cora Goodchurch opened it, and her brother Andrew peered around the door.

"I say, ladies, you are making the gentlemen frightfully jealous," he said. "We hear peals of laughter and shrieks of triumph, and we don't think it quite fair. I'm sure you have a secret tribe of elves helping you."

"Here is our elf," Sallie called, gesturing toward Meg. "We must confess to a bit of cheating, I'm afraid."

Andrew frowned. "Well, we might possibly forgive you, if you'll allow Miss March to help the gentlemen with a few final touches."

Lily's face was a mask of disapproval, but before she could speak, Cora Goodchurch took charge.

"Enter then!" Cora said gaily. "Fair is fair."

The young men crowded into the morning room. They had wound sheets around their evening clothes and one had made a crown of ivy that slipped around one ear, but their costumes looked rather sad next to those of the girls.

A young man appeared in front of Meg. "I'm Pan," he said. "Will you help me?"

"You lack a certain goatish look," Meg told him, keeping a straight face. "Perhaps some fur? And a pipe. You must have a pipe to play."

Now Meg sent the young men scurrying through the house. "Pan" took off for the schoolroom, to look for a musical pipe. "Pluto" went off in search of black cape. And Meg gladly agreed to help "Icarus," Andrew Goodchurch, with his pair of wings.

"And we'll need some candle wax," she advised him. "Remember, you flew too close to the sun, and that is what made your wings melt."

"Quite so," Andrew said. "And then I fell into the sea. I suppose if I were truly authentic I would appear dripping with salt water, but I fear for Miss Pomeray's fine carpet."

Meg laughed as she pinned and straightened. She was now in the center of a happy crowd. She tried not to notice how Lily watched her with jealous eyes.

"Miss March has helped us all so much," Andrew suddenly cried in a loud voice. "Surely she should join in the festivities!"

"What a capital idea!" another young man cheered, and the ladies joined in.

Underneath her ivy crown, Lily's face was like a mask. She laughed shrilly. "Yes, by all means, Miss March must join us. Surely there is an appropriate part she can play—a servant girl, perhaps?"

Meg's face flushed. Lily had meant to insult her. Those who had caught her words glanced at Meg, then quickly looked away.

Andrew stepped forward. "I think there is one slip of paper left in the bowl," he said in a strong, clear voice. "I'm sure it will be the name of the best and most powerful goddess of all."

Cora ran to the table and picked up the silver bowl. "Yes, Miss March, you must choose. Perhaps you'll receive Helen of Troy. I was longing for it."

"That would be appropriate," said the young man who played Pan. "For Miss March is surely capable of launching a thousand ships."

Before Meg could move, Lily rushed forward. "Let *me* choose for Miss March," she said. She reached in the bowl, then unfolded the paper. She let out a harsh laugh. "Medusa! Now *this* is perfection itself! Andrew, you must run out to the garden. We need snakes for Miss March's hair!"

The room fell silent. Lily's mocking tone shocked the group. Hot tears gathered in Meg's throat. She had weathered disappointments and snubs in her life, but never such outright cruelty as this. What had she done to merit such an enemy? Meg willed her legs to move, to carry her from the room and away from that harsh, mocking voice and her own humiliation.

Behind her she heard the rustle of Sallie's dress

as she stepped forward. Sallie plucked the paper from a surprised Lily's hand.

"I have a better idea," she called. She reached up, unclasped the garnet brooch and slowly unwound the flame-colored cloth. "I think the part of Hestia suits Meg much better. With her warmth and care of us, she is a true goddess of the hearth. I shall play Medusa."

CHAPTER THIRTEEN

A Silver Bowl

*M*eg and Sallie quickly went to work on Sallie's costume. They created a headdress of snakes fashioned from green and silver paper. A scarlet robe covered Sallie's dress and a thick gold belt showed off her slender waist.

"I declare, Sallie, I never knew you could look so fierce," Meg said, stepping back to admire her.

"And you look the very picture of sweetness," Sallie said, impulsively pressing Meg's hand.

"Come. The music has begun, and I feel like dancing."

Sallie's kind gesture had earned her the respect of all the young gentlemen. Suddenly her bright smiles and quick wit were at the heart of the festivities. One gentleman after another asked her to dance, and she whirled around the floor, losing a few of her paper snakes in the process.

Flushed with her unaccustomed popularity, Sallie bounced about, all smiles and giddy laughter. She was the belle of the ball.

Meg was happy to see her friend shine. She did not lack for partners herself. But she saw that Lily was at times forced to sit out a dance. Her face was a thundercloud.

While Meg waited for her escort to bring her a glass of punch, Sallie hurried to her side. She took a piece of paper from her pocket.

"Meg, look," she said, pressing the paper into Meg's hand. "I only just opened it. This is the paper Lily took from the bowl."

Meg unwrapped the paper. On it was written *Helen of Troy* in a clear hand.

"We should expose her," Sallie said. "It was a frightful lie. She meant to embarrass you, Meg."

"But she did not succeed," Meg said, "thanks to you, Sallie."

Sallie shook her headful of snakes. "Still, it was too cruel. I am going to tell Cora Goodchurch and her brother. Our dear hostess deserves to be exposed!"

Meg put a hand on Sallie's arm. "Please don't, Sallie. It wouldn't be right." Then, with a glance at an unhappy Lily, alone in a corner, Meg added softly, "I think she has suffered the punishment of an envious heart. She has tried to diminish the object of her jealousy, but instead she has humiliated herself."

Sallie seemed determined at first, but her persistence faded amid the warmth of laughter, music, and dancing.

After another hour of festivities, the evening came to a close at last. Everyone wrote out their choice for the best costume of the evening, and the results were placed in the silver bowl.

Meg stood back as Lily's father stepped up to the silver bowl. Although it was clear that Lily was enamored of the jovial Mr. Pomeray, his business in Europe took him away from Concord nearly half of

the year. And Lily had no brothers or sisters. No dear aunts or kind uncles to care for her. . . .

It was hard to imagine Lily all alone, holding her own with a handful of servants in this huge house.

Mr. Pomeray picked out a slip of paper. No one was surprised when he announced that Sallie Gardiner as "Medusa" had won the grand prize.

Blushing, Sallie took the silver bowl filled with roses from Mr. Pomeray. While all the guests applauded, she swept the roses from the bowl and deposited them in Meg's arms.

Meg didn't hesitate. She plucked one perfect bloom from the bouquet, crossed the room, and handed it to her hostess, Lily Pomeray.

CHAPTER FOURTEEN

Sporting Meg

"Well, I must say that you were a good sport, and that's the most important thing." Jo was, as usual, the first to speak after Meg told her story to her family on Saturday afternoon.

Meg had hurried away from the Pomeray manor that morning. Lily had pressed her to stay, but the delights of a sleigh ride were nothing compared to where Meg now knew her duty—and her pleasure— lay. She had just enough time to return and take her part in the March family theatrical.

Meg's recital of her troubles had to take place amid the cheerful chaos of preparation. The sisters were struggling into their costumes, Marmee was mending the curtain, and Laurie, dressed in his costume, had to leave in the middle to fetch the neighborhood children in a caravan of the Laurence estate's carts and carriages.

"You acted with great kindness, Meg," Marmee told her as she sewed a rip in the curtain. "And she certainly provoked you. The Pomeray girl must be quite unhappy to have treated you that way."

"That's what I thought," Meg said as she hung strings of beads round her neck for Audacia's costume. The Pomeray mansion was quite grand, but all the wealth in the world would not change the circumstances of Lily's life. Meg was grateful for her own loving, caring family. "Do you think I was right to leave the house party early?"

"Quite right," Marmee said. "There was no need to stay."

"Well, you'll miss a grand sleigh ride today, I'm sure," Amy said with a sigh, fingering her paper sword. "The snow last night and this morning is so lovely. But I am glad you are home with us, Meg."

"Lily did press me to stay with some warmth,"

Meg told them. "But I'm not sure how much her friendliness had to do with the fact that Cora and her brother were standing near."

"I prefer to think that you won her heart because you're so kind and dear," Beth said, her eyes shining underneath the black pirate hat she wore. "It was just like you to give her that rose, Meg."

"Meg was much kinder than I would have been," Jo said, striding about in her high leather boots. "Perhaps I would have wrestled myself into forgiving her. But I could not imagine bestowing a flower on her. Especially when a hearty kick would be more in order," Jo finished with fiendish satisfaction, eyeing her stout boots.

Meg hid her smile. She had seen how Jo had tried to control the explosion inside. Jo had turned all shades of red during Meg's recital of her tale. She could not bear the thought of anyone slighting Meg.

"Well, I've bundled up all the French magazines and given them back to Laurie," Meg announced. "I'm done with fuss and feathers and trying to be French!"

"Jolly good," Jo agreed, clapping Meg on the back and dislodging the elaborate hat of crushed black paper Meg was wearing.

114

"But how terrible it must have been to have to *sublimate* yourself and be a servant," Amy said with a sigh.

"*Subjugate,* you goose," Jo corrected. "And Meg didn't bend to Lily's will. She maintained her dignity and her sweetness. That's the moral of the story."

Marmee's needle paused as she gave Amy a knowing look. "A servant who does her duty well and cheerfully is no disgrace, miss," she said crisply. "Which is more than I can say for you, some days."

"And she did agree to let you attend the party in the end, Meg," Beth pointed out.

"As a Gorgon," Jo said, referring to the fearsome mythological creature. "You should have played Medusa, after all, Meg. Perhaps you could have turned Lily Pomeray to stone!"

Meg finished lacing up her kid boots. "Well, I did my best to maintain my dignity and fulfill my promise," she concluded. "And it was kind of Sallie to stand up to Lily, you must admit. As for me, I learned a lesson about envy. It can only be harbored in an unhappy heart. And such sadness can reside even in a rich house with all sorts of fine things."

Marmee smiled at Meg affectionately. "A good lesson."

"The thing is," Meg continued thoughtfully, "I realize now that I wasn't envious of Lily, really. Or even the things she has. My wish was for a return to a time I can barely remember—when ease and plenty were part of this house. But," she added quickly, "what I know now is that ease and plenty *are* a part of this house. Perhaps not in worldly riches, but in more important ways. After visiting that cold Pomeray house, I saw how truly blessed I am."

Meg looked around at the March living room, now in cheerful disarray due to the upcoming production. "I shall try never to lose sight of that again."

"And it is always better to forgive our enemies, isn't it, Marmee?" Beth asked.

Marmee nodded. "Especially when, underneath all that satin, our enemies are just frightened little girls."

"Little girls!" Jo cried, popping up from the sofa. "Christopher Columbus, look at the time! Our audience shall be arriving any minute, and we must finish dressing, and lay out the costumes for the second act, and arrange the chairs, and the curtain isn't finished—"

Marmee held up the red cloth she was hemming. "Here is the curtain, Jo. Two more stitches and I'll be done. And Hannah and I will arrange the chairs."

"Bless you, Marmee," Jo said. "Are you ready, girls? The March Family Theater is about to open its doors!"

Somehow everything was in place when the children arrived. Beth's fingers flew along the piano keys as she played a sprightly march for the children's entrance. Laurie, in a drooping mustache and beard, led the children to their seats with jokes and dramatic flourishes that sent them into peals of laughter.

Jo peeked through the curtain. "Capital! We have a full house," she announced in a whisper. Then she leaned out a little farther. "Well, I'll be, Meg, guess who is here—Sallie Gardiner!"

"Sallie?" Meg hurried forward, her red cape trailing behind her and her hair flying. "Why, what is Sallie doing here? She must have left the house party!"

"Good show," Jo said approvingly. "The girl is showing some sense, for a change."

"Oh, she saw me," Meg said, trying to keep out

of sight of most of the audience and trying to wave to Sallie at the same time.

Sallie came forward, leading a little girl by the hand.

"Meg, this is my cousin, Eliza Stewart," she said. "She thinks I am quite important, knowing one of the stars of the play. She begged for an introduction."

Meg shook the little girl's hand gravely. "How do you do, Miss Stewart."

Eliza gazed raptly at Meg, eyeing her flowing hair, scarlet cape, and black hat. She turned to Sallie, her blue eyes round with wonder. "Is she *really* your friend?" she asked her.

Sallie pressed her lips together, and moisture suddenly filled her eyes. She looked at Meg, her face full of question and apology.

Meg reached out to clasp Sallie's hand in her own. Feeling their friendship surge once more, she smiled warmly.

"Yes," Sallie said softly. "She is my friend. And I'm lucky to have her."

Jo popped up behind Meg. "Not as lucky as we are," she concluded.